THE MOMENT OF DECISION

"Christoph, what's going on?" Elizabeth asked quietly. "You're not really sick anymore, are you?"

Christoph lowered his eyes.

"You are right. I don't feel sick anymore," Christoph admitted. "The only thing I am sick about now is that I must go home. I don't ever want to go back to East Germany!"

"You can't be serious, Christoph!" Elizabeth exclaimed. "What about your family? They'd miss you terribly."

Christoph began to pace around the room. "They are the reason I don't want to go!" he cried. "All they do is push me to train harder. I am tired of people telling me what to do. I'm going to stay here!"

The twins looked at each other, shocked.

"Christoph," Elizabeth said, her heart pounding. "You don't mean you want to—"

"That's exactly what I mean!" Christoph interrupted. "I am going to defect, and no one can stop me!"

SWEET VALLEY TWINS

Elizabeth's New Hero

Written by
Jamie Suzanne

Created by
FRANCINE PASCAL

A BANTAM SKYLARK BOOK®
NEW YORK • TORONTO • LONDON • SYDNEY • AUCKLAND

RL 4, 008–012

ELIZABETH'S NEW HERO
A Bantam Skylark Book / October 1989

Sweet Valley High® and Sweet Valley Twins are trademarks of
Francine Pascal.

Conceived by Francine Pascal

Produced by Daniel Weiss Associates, Inc., 27 West 20th Street,
New York, NY 10011

Cover art by James Mathewuse

Skylark Books is a registered trademark of Bantam Books, a division of
Bantam Doubleday Dell Publishing Group, Inc.
Registered in U.S. Patent and Trademark Office and elsewhere.

ISBN 0-553-15753-1

Published simultaneously in the United States and Canada

Bantam Books are published by Bantam Books, a division of Bantam
Doubleday Dell Publishing Group, Inc. Its trademark, consisting of
the words "Bantam Books" and the portrayal of a rooster, is Registered
in U.S. Patent and Trademark Office and in other countries. Marca
Registrada. Bantam Books, 666 Fifth Avenue, New York, New York 10103.

PRINTED IN THE UNITED STATES OF AMERICA

O   0 9 8 7 6 5 4 3 2 1

Elizabeth's New Hero

One

◇

"It's perfect!" Jessica Wakefield exclaimed, inspecting the enormous banner lying on the gym floor of Sweet Valley Middle School. It was after school on Thursday, and the gym was almost empty.

Lila Fowler dipped her paintbrush into the can of purple paint and applied the finishing touches to the colorful sign welcoming the ten East German student gymnasts to Sweet Valley.

"I can't believe they're going to arrive tomorrow," Jessica added. "I thought the day would never come!"

A few weeks ago, it had been announced that ten boys from East Germany were coming to Sweet Valley for a week of gymnastic exhibitions and instructional clinics. They were due to arrive at Sweet Valley Airport the following evening, and many of the families in town planned to be there to welcome them.

"THE UNICORNS WELCOME YOU TO SWEET VALLEY!" the sign read in brilliant purple lettering. Purple was the favorite color of the Unicorn Club, an exclusive group made up of the most popular girls in school. Jessica and most of her friends were members.

"Looks like the Unicorns have been pretty busy the last two days," Jessica's twin sister, Elizabeth, said as she walked into the gym. "If they were giving out prizes for banners, you'd certainly come in first."

"Especially if the rest of the signs look like the one Caroline Pearce put together," Lila Fowler said, snickering. Lila was Jessica's best friend. "She'll be lucky if they let her into the airport parking lot with that horrible thing. Let's move this against the wall," she said, picking up one end of the sign. "I don't want anyone to step on it while it's drying."

With the banner tucked safely away in the corner of the gym, Jessica fastened her long golden hair back with a purple barrette.

Elizabeth stepped up and took a closer look at the sign. "It's really a pretty good sign, Jess, but does it have to be all *purple*?" She giggled. "Couldn't you have added some other colors?"

Jessica placed her hands on her hips and looked sharply at her twin. Though the girls looked identical in every way, from their long blond hair and sparkling blue-green eyes right down to their dimpled cheeks, their personalities couldn't have been more different.

Jessica was a member of both the Boosters, a cheering squad, and the Unicorn Club, two groups that Elizabeth would have nothing to do with. All the Unicorns ever talked about were boys, clothes, or girls who weren't in the group. Jessica was usually surrounded by a group of girls, mostly other Unicorns. She loved being the center of attention.

Elizabeth's favorite activities were more tranquil than her twin's. She wrote for the sixth-grade newspaper, *The Sweet Valley Sixers*, with the hope of becoming a writer someday. She adored reading mystery novels and enjoyed having long talks with her closest friends. But in spite of their differences, Elizabeth and Jessica were best friends.

"Well, it's definitely eye-catching," Elizabeth admitted with a laugh.

"You wouldn't be so critical of our banner if you saw Caroline's," Jessica assured her. "Hers may scare away the whole East German team."

When Caroline entered the gym from the art room carrying the banner, Elizabeth had to admit it was almost as bad as Jessica had said it was.

"What are those?" Lila asked, pointing to two multicolored rectangles on either end of the banner. "It looks like you spilled some paint."

Caroline frowned. "This is the East German flag and this is the American flag," she explained. "At least I used good colors," Caroline said hotly. "All that purple just blinds you."

Jessica ignored her comment and headed for the door. Lila and Elizabeth followed. When they got outside, Mary Wallace, one of the Unicorns, joined them and they all started walking home. Before they had even left the school grounds, Caroline came running after them.

"I guess everyone has heard that one of the East German students is staying at my house," she said. She ran her fingers through her long red hair and smiled smugly. "It's going to be *very* exciting."

Jessica wondered what had taken Caroline so long to remind everyone again. The Queen of

Gossip was always quick to broadcast such exciting news. In fact, ever since Caroline learned that her mother had signed up the Pearces as a host family, she had done nothing but brag about it to everyone she saw.

"You're lucky," Mary said. "I'd give anything to be in your place. It will be so interesting to have someone from another country staying at your house."

Caroline *was* lucky. Only ten student gymnasts were coming to town, and many more families than were needed had volunteered to be hosts.

The twins had added their name to the list, but unfortunately they were eleventh on the list.

"I've got lots of plans for Christoph," Caroline said.

"You know his name already?" Elizabeth asked, surprised.

"Of course," Caroline answered haughtily. "I know a lot about him. His name is Christoph Beckmann. He's thirteen years old. He comes from a small town outside of Leipzig. And from what I've heard, he's definitely going to make the East German Olympic team."

"I hope one of your plans is for him to show you what the East German flag looks like," Lila said curtly.

"Very funny," Caroline snapped.

The group had reached Caroline's house, and not a moment too soon as far as Jessica was concerned.

Moments later, Lila and Mary waved goodbye, and the twins turned up the driveway to their house.

"Hi, girls." Mrs. Wakefield greeted them cheerfully when they entered the kitchen. Then she took a sizzling roast from the oven.

"Where's Steven?" Elizabeth asked. "The roast beef has been out of the oven for fifteen seconds. I can't believe he's not trying to dig in already."

Mrs. Wakefield laughed. Steven, the twins' fourteen-year-old brother, was famous for his enormous appetite.

"Oh, he's busy upstairs looking for East German spy planes," Mr. Wakefield said, walking into the room.

The twins giggled as they began to set the table for dinner.

When Steven finally bounded down the stairs a few minutes later, he had a pair of binoculars slung around his neck.

"Uncover any secret agents yet?" Elizabeth asked when Steven sat down at the dinner table.

"All these East Germans coming to town are a

matter of national security," Steven said in a serious tone. "It's nothing to joke about."

Elizabeth shook her head. "I think it's exciting," she said. "We're going to publish a special issue of *The Sweet Valley Sixers* while the East German students are here. It's going to have personal interviews and cover the gymnastic exhibitions at school, too."

"You could interview the gymnast who's staying at Caroline's," Jessica suggested. "If she ever lets him out of the house, that is."

"Hey, that's right. One of those East Germans is staying just two houses away!" Steven said. "I'd better be on my toes."

"Is that so, 007?" Mr. Wakefield said. "I think you'd better calm down about this spy business. These students have come to Sweet Valley for a cultural exchange, not to spy on us. You're not being very open-minded."

Steven smiled sheepishly and went back to eating his dinner.

"Ms. Langberg says that a couple of the students might be good enough to make the East German Olympic team," Elizabeth said. "Wouldn't it be terrific to have a future Olympian in our very own town?"

"We might see him on TV in a few years!" Jessica chimed in.

Just then, the phone rang and Mrs. Wakefield got up to answer it.

"Oh, hi, Jean," the twins heard her say.

"Ugh!" Jessica groaned. "It's Caroline's mother. She's probably calling Mom to brag, just like Caroline."

"C'mon, Jess," Elizabeth said. "Caroline's excited about what's going on, just like everyone else in Sweet Valley. If one of the East Germans were staying here, we'd be telling everyone, too."

"No way," Jessica said. "I wouldn't be blabbing about it to everyone like Motor-Mouth Pearce."

Mrs. Wakefield hung up the phone and sat back down at the dinner table.

"Well, the Pearces have had an unfortunate change of plans," she said. "Mrs. Pearce's mother is ill, and she's afraid that next week will be much too hectic to have a guest in the house."

"Oh, no," said Elizabeth, unable to hide her disappointment. "Where will Christoph stay?"

"That may be for us to decide," Mrs. Wakefield said mysteriously.

Jessica's smile widened. "You mean he might stay *here*?"

"With us?" Steven choked out.

"Maybe," Mrs. Wakefield said. "We're next on the list of host families, remember? Mrs. Pearce is calling the rest of the welcoming committee to see if it's OK for the student to stay at our house instead."

"When will we know?" Elizabeth blurted out.

"As soon as Mrs. Pearce calls us back," their mother replied.

"I've got to call Lila!" Jessica said, jumping up from the table. "And Ellen! They're going to die when they hear!"

"Just a minute, young lady," Mr. Wakefield said. "Aren't you getting a little ahead of yourself? We're not even sure he's going to stay here. Sit down and finish your dinner."

Elizabeth laughed as Jessica sat down again. "I thought you'd be more dignified than Caroline, Jess, and not blab about it to everyone. If you start making calls, Mrs. Pearce will get a busy signal from now until midnight."

When the phone rang again a few minutes later, Jessica almost jumped out of her seat.

The twins and Steven were perched on the edge of their chairs while Mrs. Wakefield talked on the phone.

When she finally hung up, the twins were squirming with anticipation.

"Well?" Jessica cried.

"Is he going to stay with us?" Elizabeth asked excitedly.

Mrs. Wakefield smiled brightly. "He certainly is," she announced.

The twins leapt from their seats and cheered. Neither could believe how lucky they were. One of the biggest events in Sweet Valley history was about to happen, and they were going to be at the center of it!

Two

When the twins went downstairs for breakfast on Friday morning, their mother was just about to leave for work. Her part-time job as an interior designer often got her up and out of the house before the girls left for school.

"I have to meet a client, girls," she said, picking up her briefcase. "Don't forget, if we're going to meet the plane tonight, we'll have to leave as soon as your father gets home. Try not to be too late after school."

"Don't worry, Mom," Elizabeth assured her. "We wouldn't be late for this."

"Lila says the local TV station is going to be there covering the East Germans' arrival," Jessica said. "That means our Unicorn banner might be on the news."

"All right, girls. I'll see you later." Mrs. Wakefield gave each twin a hug and went outside.

At the table, Steven was finishing his breakfast. His expression was gloomy.

"Did you lose your binoculars?" Jessica teased.

Steven shook his head. "Worse than that," he said with a scowl. "I've been kicked out of my room. Mom and Dad said that Christoph would be more comfortable there. I've been banished to the pullout couch for the next week."

"That's too bad, Steven," Elizabeth said. "But I'm sure Christoph will appreciate it."

"Besides, we'll feel much safer with our very own spy patrol sleeping downstairs," Jessica added with a mischievous grin.

But Steven was obviously in no mood for joking. He didn't even crack a smile.

The twins finished breakfast, grabbed their lunch bags, and darted out of the house. When they arrived at school, several of the Unicorns were waiting anxiously out front.

As soon as Jessica had heard the good news the

night before, she had called all her friends. "Any more news?" Lila Fowler demanded as Jessica approached. "Tell me the whole story again," Ellen Riteman, a fellow club member, insisted.

Proud to be the center of attention as she walked through the crowded corridors toward homeroom, Jessica recounted the events that had taken place so far, as well as *her* plans for Christoph.

"I think a tour of Sweet Valley should be first on the list," Jessica said.

"Maybe we could ride our bicycles to the beach," Ellen suggested.

"How about going to the movies?" Janet Howell, the president of the Unicorns, added. "I'll bet they don't have horror movies in East Germany."

"And don't forget the dance next Friday night," Lila reminded them.

Elizabeth listened quietly as one suggestion followed another. She was beginning to wonder if she would get to spend any time at all with Christoph.

When Elizabeth walked into math class later that morning, she took her usual seat near the front of the room between Amy Sutton and Brooke Dennis. Amy and Brooke were two of Elizabeth's close friends and both girls worked on *The Sweet Valley Sixers* with her. She began to tell them the news about Christoph, but they had already heard.

"With Christoph at your house, I have a feeling our next issue of the *Sixers* is going to be the best ever," Amy said, her gray eyes shining.

Just then, Julie Porter came in and sat down in front of Elizabeth. Julie worked on the class paper, too. She twisted around in her seat, smiling brightly. "I think it's fantastic that Christoph is staying with you," she said. "Now we don't have to listen to Caroline talk about him all week!"

The three girls laughed. It seemed Caroline had succeeded in annoying just about everyone at school.

"Any ideas for our next issue?" Amy asked.

"We should do profiles on the gymnasts and their coaches, too," Julie said.

Elizabeth nodded enthusiastically. "I think it would be a good idea to finish it before the team leaves," she said. "That way they can take copies home with them."

"That's a great idea," Brooke agreed. "Sort of like a souvenir."

"Exactly," Elizabeth said. "It's not going to be easy, though. We don't have much time."

"You're right," Amy said. "Maybe we should

meet at lunch today and figure out who's going to write what."

"Good idea," Elizabeth said. "A head start is exactly what we're going to need."

As soon as classes were over for the day, the twins met in front of the school. Jessica had the Unicorns' banner rolled up and tucked under her arm as they walked home. She didn't trust anyone else to take care of it.

The twins arrived home just as their father was pulling into the driveway. Steven and Mrs. Wakefield came outside, and the whole family piled into the maroon van. A short while later they were walking through the crowd at the airport. Jessica spotted Lila immediately.

"Lila! Hi!" Jessica called, running over to her.

Lila was standing with Ellen Riteman and Tamara Chase. Dozens of students and parents from Sweet Valley were milling around, waiting for the plane to arrive. The mayor of Sweet Valley and several town council members were there as well.

Across the noisy waiting area, Elizabeth stood anxiously with Amy and Ken Matthews, another sixth grader at Sweet Valley Middle School. They had secured a perfect spot near the doorway to see the gymnasts as they came through Customs.

"I think they're here!" Elizabeth said.

As the crowd of onlookers began to buzz noisily, the East German students, all in their team uniforms, walked through the doorway and into the lounge, waving and smiling at everyone. Then they climbed the steps of the small stage that was set up at the far side of the room. Mr. Herbert Lodge, the mayor of Sweet Valley, a short, round man in a three-piece suit, shook hands with one of the coaches, then raised his hands to quiet the crowd.

"It is my pleasure to welcome the East German student gymnastics team to Sweet Valley," Mr. Lodge announced. Then he stepped down, and two of the town council members made short speeches.

"I wish they'd stop all this talking and let us meet Christoph," Jessica said impatiently.

Finally, Mr. Lodge began to call off the names of the host families. When the Wakefields' name was called, the whole family walked up to the side of the stage. They were met by a quiet-looking blond-haired boy. He smiled shyly and shook Mr. Wakefield's hand.

"I am Christoph Beckmann," he said in perfect English. "I am very happy to meet you."

Jessica felt as if she was going to faint. Compact and muscular, Christoph was the picture-perfect gymnast. She thought he was gorgeous. He smiled and repeated their names as they introduced themselves. Jessica stared into his clear blue eyes. Her heart started pounding.

"You must be tired from such a long flight," Mrs. Wakefield said to Christoph.

Christoph nodded and smiled wearily.

"It was a very long trip," he said. "And the food on the plane wasn't very good."

Mr. Wakefield laughed. "Then I think we should get you home quickly and feed you some real food," he said.

Once they had all gathered around the dinner table, Jessica bombarded Christoph with one question after another.

"Do you live in a house in East Germany?" she asked.

Christoph swallowed a bite of his hamburger, then dipped one of his french fries into the ketchup on his plate. It had been the twins' idea to serve him a typical American dinner for his first meal in Sweet Valley, and he seemed to love it. Steven sat across the table, keeping a watchful eye on their guest. So far, he hadn't said more than a few words to Christoph.

"Yes, but it's very different from your house," Christoph said in answer to Jessica's question. "I have a picture I can show you." He took his wallet from his pocket and showed the Wakefields a photograph of a small stone house with beautiful stained-glass windows on either side of the front door. A low, ivy-covered fence separated the front yard from a quaint, cobblestoned street.

"What's your school like?" Jessica asked, passing the picture over to Elizabeth.

"I am told it is very much like school here in America," Christoph replied. "The only difference is that we go to school almost all year long. We have only a few weeks off each year. In America, I have heard, you get all summer off to have fun."

Jessica wrinkled her nose and stared at Christoph in horror. She gasped. "No summer vacation," she gasped. "I'd go crazy."

"Do you have any brothers or sisters?" Elizabeth asked.

"I have two sisters," he said. "Gretchen and Ingrid." He passed her another photograph.

"You're lucky they're not twins," Steven joked. "Twins are twice as much trouble."

Jessica and Elizabeth shot Steven angry looks.

"Are they gymnasts, too?" Jessica asked, turning back to Christoph.

"Yes," Christoph said. "In my family we begin training at a very early age. You see, my father was a gymnast and he had very high hopes of making the Olympic team. But an injury took him out of the competition. I have been training since I was a very small boy. My father has taught me everything I know."

As he spoke, Elizabeth couldn't help noticing that Christoph's eyes suddenly had a faraway look, and his cheerful mood seemed to fade.

After dinner, everyone went into the living room. The Wakefields spent the next couple of hours talking to Christoph about his family and his country, and answering his questions about America. Only Steven didn't seem to enjoy talking to Christoph. He remained unusually quiet.

"Do you like any American sports, Christoph?" Jessica asked. "You know, like baseball or basketball . . ."

"Basketball!" Christoph exclaimed excitedly. "That's a game I'd like to learn more about."

"Maybe Steven can teach you," Elizabeth suggested. "He's one of the best players on the junior varsity team at Sweet Valley High."

"I suppose I could," Steven said reluctantly. "If you really want to learn."

"Oh, yes," Christoph said with a smile. "Can you teach me to slam dunk?"

Steven laughed. He finally seemed to be warming up to Christoph. "Even I can't do that yet," he admitted, "and I'm a lot taller than you. But I'll bet I can have you shooting foul shots like a pro in no time."

"Great," Christoph said. "When do we start?"

"We could go out back right now," Steven said, unable to hide his enthusiasm. "We've got a hoop on the side of the house, and lights, too. Let's go."

"Hold on a minute," Mrs. Wakefield said. "I'm sure Christoph is very tired. In fact, it's been a long day for all of us. A good night's sleep is definitely in order."

The twins and Steven groaned.

"Can't we stay up and talk to Christoph for just a little while longer?" Jessica pleaded.

But then Christoph yawned loudly. Everyone laughed.

"Does that answer your question?" Mr. Wakefield asked. "Up to bed, all of you!"

At the top of the stairs, Elizabeth stopped and looked back down toward the living room, where she saw Steven helping Christoph with his suitcases. She nudged Jessica, and they smiled at each other.

"Looks like the spy watcher has softened up," Elizabeth whispered to her twin.

"I'll say," Jessica replied with a laugh. "That didn't take long. A little basketball talk sure goes a long way with Steven."

Three

◇

"Christoph must still be sleeping," Jessica whispered to Elizabeth. They were standing outside the door to Steven's room. "He really must have been exhausted."

It was ten o'clock on Saturday morning, and the twins were trying to decide how to spend the day with their visitor. Each member of the East German team was allowed to spend the weekend with his host family, doing whatever he wanted.

"All the Unicorns are going to meet at the Dairi Burger at one o'clock," Jessica said. "I *have* to bring Christoph."

"Jess, there's a whole week to go to the Dairi Burger," Elizabeth said. "Amy and I have a deadline for the *Sixers*. It would really help if we could interview Christoph today."

"Oh, come on, Elizabeth," Jessica whined. "The Unicorns are counting on me."

"Why don't we let Christoph decide what he wants to do?" Elizabeth suggested. "I think that's fair."

"OK," Jessica said haughtily. "We'll let Christoph decide." But she knew that if she were given the choice between a boring interview and a fabulous time at the Dairi Burger, the Dairi Burger would win hands down.

The twins tiptoed quietly past Steven's room and down the stairs. When they walked into the kitchen, they were shocked. It looked as though a hurricane had hit. Dishes were piled in the sink, and cereal boxes and milk and juice cartons littered the table. Mr. and Mrs. Wakefield were busily cleaning up.

"I never thought I'd see another appetite to match Steven's," Mrs. Wakefield said, shaking her head.

"I'm glad we had twin girls and not twin boys," Mr. Wakefield said, dropping an empty box into the trash can. "I'd need a second job just to keep the family fed."

The twins looked at each other in confusion.

"Look!" Elizabeth said to Jessica. She pointed out the window. Christoph was outside, shooting baskets with Steven.

"What time did Christoph get up?" Jessica asked in amazement.

"Oh, they were up long before we were," Mr. Wakefield said. "We had to beg them to come in for breakfast." He glanced at the dishes in the sink. "Now I'm almost sorry we did."

A few minutes later, Steven came into the house for a drink. "Christoph's a pretty good basketball player," he said, smiling devilishly. He gulped down a glass of milk as fast as he could.

"Don't think you're going to play basketball with him all day," Jessica warned. "I'm bringing him to the Dairi Burger this afternoon."

"Don't worry, we're not playing basketball all day," Steven replied. "We're going to the football game at school in a little while. Christoph's never been to a football game. Guess you'll have to make other plans, Jess," he added as he shot out the door again.

Jessica shook her head. "Yesterday morning, Steven thought Christoph was a spy," she moaned. "Today they're best friends."

"I don't know about you, but I think I'll go to

the football game, too," Elizabeth said. "I'm sure Christoph will answer a few questions for my interview while he watches the game. Besides, it sounds like fun."

"Oh, I guess I'll come, too," Jessica said, sounding disappointed. "But what am I supposed to tell the Unicorns?" The weekend wasn't going the way she'd planned, and it was clear there was nothing she could do about it.

"Can we sit at the top?" Christoph asked when they arrived at the football field. "I want to be sure to see everything." He looked around as he stood in the last row of the bleachers.

When the game started, Christoph listened intently as Steven explained the rules and what was happening on the field. "The object is to get the ball in the end zone of the other team," Steven said right after the opening kickoff.

Christoph looked confused. "But where is the net?" he asked. "How do you know if you get the ball into the end zone if you don't have a net?"

Steven laughed. "Oh, you mean like soccer," he said. "In American football, all you have to do is cross the line and you get six points."

"Six points!" Christoph repeated with amazement. "In my country, they give only one point. I like your game much better! You get many more points!"

During halftime, Jessica sat next to Elizabeth and pouted.

"What happened to Christoph the Spy?" Jessica said sarcastically to Steven when Christoph went to get something to drink. "I thought you were going to watch his every move. "

Steven laughed and shook his head. "I don't know what you're talking about," he said. "You two are more of a threat to national security than Christoph. We're friends."

"Cheer up, Jess," Elizabeth said. "I'm sure you'll get to spend plenty of time with him."

The game remained exciting right to the end. Sweet Valley High made a touchdown pass in the final seconds, for a 27 to 24 victory.

"You should feel lucky, Christoph," Steven said as they climbed down from the bleachers. They headed toward the parking lot where Mrs. Wakefield was waiting to take them to the Valley Mall. "You may have seen the most exciting game all year."

"I just hope the rest of my trip is as much fun as this," Christoph said.

A couple of hours later, the twins, Steven, and

Christoph were sitting in a booth at Casey's Place, an old-fashioned ice cream parlor at the Valley Mall. They had made the rounds of the mall, showing Christoph all of their favorite shops, and for dinner had eaten a pizza—Christoph's first one.

"There are so many stores in this mall," Christoph said. He was eating a Super-Double Banana Split Special, but even with some help from Steven he couldn't finish the jumbo-sized treat. Most of the ice cream was still sitting in his dish, melting. "Are there any more stores here?"

"No, you've seen them all," Jessica said, laughing. "You were amazing. You went into every store in the mall in less than two hours. Even *I've* never done that."

"Well, do we have time to do anything else?" Christoph asked.

The twins were exhausted from all the walking they had done that afternoon. But Christoph appeared to be as fresh as he was that morning.

"What time is it?" Jessica asked.

"Seven o'clock," Elizabeth answered, looking at her watch.

"We could see a movie, " Steven suggested. "*Danger Alley* is playing at the Valley Cinema!"

"That sounds great," Christoph said. "We don't get to see many American movies in East Germany. When I get back home, I'll be able to tell my friends all about it." He smiled. "This is terrific—a football game, the mall, and a movie all in one day. This is much better than practicing gymnastics."

As they walked to the theater, Elizabeth silently wondered why Christoph had made that remark about gymnastics. Didn't he like practicing his routines? Could it be possible that Christoph's first love wasn't gymnastics?

On Sunday afternoon, the twins, Steven, and Christoph were in Steven's room, listening to records and introducing Christoph to the latest American music.

Christoph tapped his fingers on the edge of Steven's dresser, keeping perfect time to the music that was blaring from the stereo. Even without drumsticks, Christoph's fingers beat out a rhythm to the rock songs, performing drumrolls as intricate as those on the records.

"Wow! Do you play the drums?" Steven asked. He was lying down on the floor on his sleeping bag. After sleeping the first night on the pullout couch, Steven was now sharing his room with Christoph.

Christoph shook his head. "I have an old drum

set at home. It's not a very good one, but I love to play it when I get the chance, which isn't very often. My gymnastics training takes up most of my time. But I would love to play in a band some-day," he said.

"Who's your favorite American rock star?" Jessica asked. "Mine is Melody Power. She's outrageous!"

Elizabeth rolled her eyes. Lately, Jessica had become a Melody Power fanatic. One whole wall of her room was covered with her posters.

"I like lots of American bands," Christoph an-swered, his eyes lighting up. "Especially Johnny Buck! I've got both of his albums."

"Both?" Jessica said quizzically. "Johnny Buck has six albums out already. His latest just came out last week."

"Do you have any of them?" Christoph asked excitedly. "I'd love to hear them. It's not so easy to get American records in my country."

"We've got every one except the new one, *Sat-urday Night Dancin'*," Jessica said, rummaging through Steven's record collection. "Valley Sounds sold out every copy the first day it was in the store. They're supposed to get more pretty soon."

Jessica found an album that Christoph hadn't heard before and slipped it on the turntable. Even though the songs were unfamiliar to Christoph, he felt the rhythm of the songs and tapped out a lively beat.

"You really are good," Elizabeth said. "If you're half as good a gymnast as you are a drummer, you're definitely going to make the Olympics."

"I hope I'm a better gymnast," Christoph said, suddenly turning serious. "My parents will be very disappointed if I don't make the Olympic team. For them, I must be more than a good gymnast. I must be the *best*!"

"Don't your parents let you do anything else besides practice gymnastics?" Steven asked.

"Not really," Christoph said, his face growing red. "To them, gymnastics is everything. And to be the best you have to practice hard all the time."

They listened to the rest of the album without saying another word. Elizabeth felt sorry for Christoph. She couldn't imagine what it would be like to practice one thing all day long. It took that sort of dedication to get to the Olympics, but she wasn't convinced that that was what Christoph really wanted.

Suddenly, Mrs. Wakefield opened the door. Behind her were two of Christoph's teammates. Elizabeth recognized them from the airport.

"Excuse me," Mrs. Wakefield said. "You've got a couple of visitors. Bruno and Konrad."

The two boys walked into Steven's room, nodded and said hello. Bruno, the taller of the two,
glanced at Elizabeth. His dark, piercing eyes made
her uncomfortable. Konrad was the same height
as Christoph, with the same muscular frame and
friendly eyes.

"Tomorrow's practice is at nine A.M. sharp,"
Bruno said. "As you know, Coach Schmidt does
not tolerate lateness. Here is the schedule of exhibitions as well," Bruno added, handing Christoph
a sheet of paper. "Tomorrow we will be at the
middle school, performing for the gym classes all
day."

"Would you like to sit down?" Elizabeth asked.

Konrad nodded and sat down next to Christoph
on Steven's bed.

"I'd love to listen to some records," Konrad
said.

But Bruno frowned and shook his head. "Working out is much more important than listening to
music." He looked straight at Christoph. "You
should spend more time practicing, Christoph. Listening to music will not help you get to the
Olympics."

With that, Bruno turned and walked out of the
room.

Four

◇

"We waited at the Dairi Burger until four o'clock!" Lila Fowler said to Jessica first thing on Monday morning. "You could have at least called!"

Jessica shrugged. Ever since she arrived at school, she had been trying to explain what had happened on Saturday. But the rest of the Unicorns were so upset about being stood up she hadn't been able to explain.

"By the time we realized that you weren't coming," Tamara Chase said hotly, "it was too late to make it to the game!"

"Yeah, instead, we spent hours sitting around

the Dairi Burger," Janet Howell hissed. "We wasted the whole day. And then you didn't even bother to call us yesterday!"

They all looked at Jessica with fire in their eyes.

"We didn't do that much yesterday," Jessica mumbled. She had tried to think up an excuse all morning. The truth was that in all the commotion she had simply forgotten to tell them that she wouldn't be coming.

"Hi, everybody," a voice called from behind them.

Jessica turned around to see Christoph. He smiled warmly. He was wearing a new pair of jeans he had bought at the mall, and was carrying a leather gym bag.

"You must be part of the famous Unicorn Club," he said. "Jessica told me all about you. I've never heard of a Unicorn Club. I was anxious to meet you."

Lila, Janet, Ellen, and Tamara glanced at each other. The scowls they wore only seconds before were now replaced with glowing smiles.

Jessica breathed a sigh of relief as she quickly introduced everyone to Christoph. In no time at all, the Unicorns had forgotten about the Dairi Burger incident. Christoph was an immediate hit.

"I am sorry you weren't at the football game on Saturday," Christoph said. "It was a very hectic day."

"We heard," Janet gushed. "Why don't we go to the Dairi Burger after school today? That is, if you don't already have plans."

"That sounds great," Christoph said.

"I'll bet this is going to be a very busy week for you, Christoph," Ellen said. She had nudged her way in front of Lila so she could be close to him. Like the other Unicorns, she couldn't keep her eyes off of him.

"I will be pretty busy," Christoph responded. "We have exhibitions in all the gym classes in the middle school today. Then we do the same thing at the high school tomorrow. We are here to demonstrate gymnastics, but we are also here to make friends and experience the American way of life. I am looking forward to that most of all."

"Well, if you stick with us, you'll have a wonderful time here in America," Lila assured him.

"Great!" Christoph said. "Well, I must go practice now. I will see you during your gym classes."

The Unicorns stared dreamily at Christoph as he walked down the hall, their anger at Jessica completely forgotten.

*   *   *

During gym class that day, the twins sat together on the bleachers. On the floor, the East German gymnasts were finishing their warm-up drills.

The team's head coach, a short, bald man with a handlebar mustache, was pacing back and forth in front of them. The two assistant coaches stood on either side of the team.

"May I have your attention, please!" Ms. Langberg, the girls' gym teacher, called out. "Let's show Coach Schmidt and the East German gymnastics team how happy we are that they've come to Sweet Valley!"

An enormous cheer erupted from the students in the bleachers. When the exhibition began, the crowd continued to cheer. It was hard to believe that the gymnasts, some the same age as the twins, were able to perform such fantastic routines. Each of the members of the East German squad performed on the rings, side horse, horizontal bar, and long horse. Both Elizabeth and Jessica thought Christoph was the best gymnast on the team.

"Amazing!" Jessica cried as Christoph performed a difficult twisting dismount from the side horse. She jumped up and cheered wildly.

Christoph caught sight of Jessica and waved before taking a bow.

"The parallel bars will be the final event of to-day's exhibition," Ms. Langberg announced. "Coach Schmidt has suggested that we treat it as a compe-tition, so that you can see how an event is scored. Two of the students will compete against each other. Coach Schmidt, the assistant coaches, and I will be the judges. We'll award each gymnast a score out of ten points. The higher the number, the better the performance."

Coach Schmidt walked down the line and se-lected Christoph and Bruno to compete against each other.

Bruno went first. His serious expression made it clear he thought of this as more than just an exhi-bition. He mounted the bars and spun through his routine with blinding speed. His muscles strained and sweat beaded his brow. By the time he con-cluded his routine with a magnificent somersault dismount, the crowd was on its feet and cheer-ing.

Ms. Langberg, Coach Schmidt, and one of the assistant coaches each awarded Bruno a 9.8. The other assistant coach gave the routine a 9.9, al-most a perfect score.

The twins saw Bruno smile for the first time. He raised his hand triumphantly in the air.

"Do you think Christoph even has a chance of getting a better score than Bruno?" Jessica wondered out loud. As much as she hated to admit it, Bruno's performance had been terrific.

But Christoph's smooth and fluid movements quickly erased all her doubts. His flawless spins, twists, and turns delighted the crowd, who responded with thundering applause.

After his perfectly executed dismount, Christoph turned to the crowd and took a bow. Jessica glanced at Elizabeth. Both girls had their fingers crossed.

One of the assistant coaches awarded Christoph a 9.8, the same score he had given Bruno. But when the other three judges' cards displayed 9.9's, the entire gym burst into a deafening roar.

"He won! He won!" Elizabeth shouted.

Jessica jumped up on her seat, whistling and waving wildly at Christoph.

Coach Schmidt shook hands with Bruno, then raised Christoph's arm high in the air, signaling victory. Christoph displayed a friendly smile as he approached his opponent, but Bruno, scowling menacingly, pushed Christoph roughly out of his way and stormed out of the gym into the locker room.

The entire group went silent. Everyone was shocked by his display of poor sportsmanship.

Elizabeth and Jessica stared at each other in disbelief. It was clear that Bruno was terribly jealous of Christoph. And Elizabeth had an awful feeling that this wasn't the end of the trouble between them.

Five

◇

"Wow! You've been all over the world!" Elizabeth said to Christoph. She wrote furiously in her notebook. The twins, Amy, and Christoph were sitting in a booth at the Dairi Burger after school on Monday afternoon.

"I've been on the squad since I was eight years old," Christoph said. "Last year we visited France and England and the Soviet Union." He took a sip of his chocolate milkshake. "But this is the first time I have come to America. I like it here very much. It is very different from my country."

"What do you like most about America?" Elizabeth asked.

"Everyone seems a lot more relaxed here," Christoph said, looking around the room. "In Germany, people are so formal."

"You make it sound as if you don't like it where you live," Elizabeth said.

"Oh, I do," Christoph replied uneasily. "It's just that being here in America has made me realize how different my life is. I really like it here."

"Well, maybe after you tell your parents how much you like it here, things at home will be different," Amy suggested.

Christoph shrugged. "Maybe," he said.

Elizabeth closed her notebook. In less than an hour, she had almost four pages of notes for her article on Christoph. "I've got to go," she said, getting up. "I'm going straight home to write up this article so I can hand it in to Mr. Bowman tomorrow. I'll call you when I'm finished, Amy. Thanks again, Christoph. I'll see you later."

A few minutes after Elizabeth had left, Lila, Ellen, and Janet walked in and quickly slid into the booth.

"You were fabulous at the exhibition today," Ellen said to Christoph.

"It was just a demonstration," Christoph said

shyly. "I save my best moves for the competition."

"I still thought it was fantastic," Ellen gushed.

"Hey, look who's here," Lila said to Christoph. "Aren't they on your team?"

Christoph's eyes brightened. "Of course," he said, waving to the three boys who had just entered the Dairi Burger. The boys walked over, and Christoph introduced them.

"This is Viktor," Christoph said. Viktor smiled and waved to the girls. "And this is Dieter and Hans," Christoph added, pointing to the two other boys.

Dieter and Viktor pulled a table over and placed it at the end of the booth. The three boys went up to the counter and returned a few minutes later with ice cream sodas. Jessica looked around the table happily. Everyone was laughing and talking.

"I can't believe this!" Lila said to Jessica, after two more gymnasts, Oskar and Max, had come into the Dairi Burger and joined them. "This is turning into the social event of the year!"

"We heard that the Dairi Burger was the best place to go," Max said. Like the other members of the team, he was compact and powerfully built. He had bright blue eyes and short blond hair. "This place is terrific!"

"Who are you staying with, Viktor?" Ellen asked. Viktor was the smallest boy on the team, and one of the friendliest.

"I'm staying at Randy's house," Viktor said. Randy Mason was the sixth-grade class president. "He had some homework to do, but he said he'd be here later."

"So, does everyone like Sweet Valley?" Jessica asked.

"It's great!" Dieter said.

"I think I would like to live here," Christoph said. "Everything here is perfect, not just the weather."

Dieter suddenly turned and stared at Christoph.

"How can you say that?" he said. "All your friends and family are at home."

"I enjoy it here very much," Christoph answered firmly. "I like everything here so far. And I am sure there are other things that are interesting as well."

"Like the beach," Viktor chimed in. "When can we go there? I'd like to see some surfing."

Christoph smiled. "Me, too! I've never seen anybody ride the waves."

Jessica thought for a moment. "Do you guys have an exhibition after school tomorrow?"

"We're doing demonstrations during gym classes

at the high school tomorrow," Christoph said. "Then there's a gymnastics clinic after school. But that shouldn't last too long. We can go right after we're finished with that."

"Then let's hit the beach tomorrow!" Lila said.

"OK!" Dieter shouted.

Just then Lila whispered, "Oh, no! Look who's here!"

Jessica's heart dropped. Bruno was coming through the front door of the Dairi Burger. He was the last person in the world Jessica wanted to see.

As soon as Bruno caught sight of Christoph and his other teammates, he strode over and glared at them.

The noisy chatter stopped as Bruno spoke to Christoph in German. Several of the other gymnasts laughed quietly as Bruno spoke. And though Jessica couldn't understand a word that Bruno was saying, it was obvious that Christoph didn't think it was funny at all.

"What did he say?" Jessica asked Viktor when Bruno had stopped talking.

"He said Christoph should spend more time training and less time flirting!" Viktor whispered. "Bruno is just jealous of Christoph. Christoph is the number one gymnast on our team, but he still likes to have fun."

Christoph quickly stood up, unable to hide his anger any longer. "I train as hard as everyone else!" he shouted at Bruno. "You should spend more time worrying about yourself than about how much I practice. I am still better than you are, and I proved it once again today!"

Jessica's heart was racing. She thought for a moment that Bruno might hit Christoph. But instead, Bruno just gave a sinister smile.

"I am sorry that the party has to end this way," Christoph said to everyone at the table. "Now I must leave."

"Oh, please stay, Christoph," Jessica pleaded. "We're having such a great time."

"You're our guest of honor," Ellen said. "You can't leave."

But Christoph turned and marched quickly out of the Dairi Burger, leaving everyone stunned. Suddenly Jessica realized that he would never be able to find his way home. She jumped up and ran out after him, casting a furious glance at Bruno as she passed.

"Christoph, wait!" Jessica called, finally catching up with him a block away from the Dairi Burger.

"I am very sorry. I am sure I have ruined the

party," Christoph said as they walked. He frowned and shook his head.

"It's not your fault," Jessica assured him. "It's that creep, Bruno. Why is he so mean?"

Christoph sighed. "Bruno thinks that everyone should be like him: all work and no play. It is true what Viktor said—Bruno is jealous because I am better than he is. I used to offer to help him, but not anymore. He thinks that everyone should train hard all the time. I work hard, but I also like to relax sometimes."

"But why do you care what Bruno thinks?" Jessica asked, confused.

"It's not what Bruno thinks that worries me," Christoph answered anxiously. "He threatens to tell my parents that I have not been working hard. He says that if I am not careful on this trip, he will tell my father. That would be disastrous. My father is very much like Bruno. He thinks that training for the Olympics is everything. I want to make the Olympics, but I also want to enjoy my trip to America."

"But the exhibitions don't mean *that* much, do they?" Jessica asked. "I mean, they're only practice, right?"

"Yes, that is true," Christoph said. "But Coach Schmidt told us all that the exhibition on Thursday will be a competition to see who is the best overall gymnast on the team. Coach Schmidt said we should treat it as if it were the trials for the Olympics. That competition will be very important. I must make sure that I do well that day."

As they passed the Mello Music Store, Christoph stopped. In the window was a shining new drum set. Christoph stared at the drums for a moment, the sadness and anger suddenly gone from his face.

But when they continued on toward home, the sadness returned once again. Jessica felt sorry for him. A week was a very short time, and Christoph was trying his best to make his trip here a happy one.

Obviously he's not going to be able to do it alone, Jessica thought. *It's up to Elizabeth and me to help!*

By the time Elizabeth and Julie found the gym at Sweet Valley High after school on Tuesday, the instructional clinic was in full swing. They had agreed to meet Jessica, Steven, Christoph and his friends from the team, and several of the Unicorns at the high school so they could all ride bikes to the beach when the clinic was over.

"I didn't think so many kids were interested in gymnastics," Elizabeth said, looking out over the crowded gym. There were several sets of parallel bars, pommel horses, and horizontal bars scattered around the floor, with dozens of high school students being shown how to use them.

"How are we ever going to find Christoph in this place?" Julie asked, glancing around at all the people.

"Easy," Elizabeth said confidently. "All we have to do is look for a blur of purple." She spotted the Unicorns and Christoph over on the other side of the gym.

"Hi, everybody," Elizabeth said as she and Julie walked up to them.

The Unicorns waved hello and went back to watching Christoph demonstrate a vault on the long horse. He sprinted across the mat, gaining speed. His feet hit the springboard in front of the horse with a powerful thud. Then, as he flew through the air his hands hit the horse and he vaulted himself over, twisting and spinning until he hit the ground on the other side.

"You should see the move Christoph can do on the parallel bars," Steven said. "He demonstrated it today during my gym class." He shook his head, as if he had never seen anything so amazing. "Why don't you show them?" he asked.

"Wow! That was great!" Elizabeth exclaimed.

Christoph shrugged. "I don't think I should," he said. "I'm supposed to be teaching, not demonstrating."

"Oh, please. Can't you show us . . . just once?" Lila Fowler asked.

"Please, Christoph," Jessica chimed in. "The clinic's almost over."

Elizabeth looked around the noisy gym. Coach Schmidt was busy showing several Sweet Valley students a move on the pommel horse. She hoped they weren't pressuring Christoph into doing something he shouldn't do.

"I guess it can't hurt to show you," Christoph said. "I like to practice the move whenever I can anyway."

He hopped onto the parallel bars and swung his legs back and forth, gathering momentum for his dismount. When he performed the dismount, a magnificent twisting back flip, the crowd watching him let out a cheer of approval. Christoph smiled and gave a short wave to the onlookers.

"That was wonderful!" Elizabeth exclaimed.

"He's the only one on the team who can do that move," Steven explained proudly.

Suddenly, Coach Schmidt walked up to Christoph, an angry look on his face. "We are not here to show off, Christoph," he said sternly. "You should know better than that. I have been getting very unfavorable reports about you lately."

Christoph lowered his eyes in shame.

"You are part of a team," Coach Schmidt added. "You are not here to make yourself look better than the others. I hope you are on your best behavior for the rest of the trip."

When the coach had finished, Christoph took his place at the long horse once again. He watched silently as several students took turns vaulting.

Elizabeth felt horrible. Christoph had only performed the move because they had asked him to, not so he could show off to the crowd. She wanted to tell Coach Schmidt, but before she could say anything he had turned and walked away.

Six

◇

"Wow!" Max cried happily. "That wave looks like a tunnel!"

The twins and Steven laughed as Christoph, Max, and Oskar raced toward the water at the beach. The surf was up, and the waves were crashing thunderously onto the shore. Dozens of surfers, wearing brightly colored wet suits, were riding the waves and paddling out to sea.

"It looks like the beach was just what Christoph needed," Jessica said, relieved. As soon as the gymnastics clinic had ended, they had headed for the beach.

Christoph came running up, his hair dripping wet. He sat down next to the twins on a beach towel.

"The beach is great," he said, wiggling his toes in the sand. "I wish we had beaches like this at home. The more I see of Sweet Valley the more I like it."

"Do you think Coach Schmidt is angry at you?" Elizabeth asked. She hoped Christoph wasn't in too much trouble.

"I don't think he's very angry," Christoph said. "And even if he is, I know what will make him happy again."

"What?" Steven asked.

"Tomorrow night is the special exhibition at the middle school. All of Sweet Valley will be there. I'm going to do my new dismount on the parallel bars. Once he sees how well I can perform that move, he will see that I am taking this very seriously. A great performance always makes Coach Schmidt happy."

"I think you're right, Christoph," Steven said. "That's the way it works on the basketball team, too."

"If I can perform to perfection, it will prove to him that I am still the best."

*　　*　　*

Christoph held up a navy blue T-shirt and looked at Jessica, Lila, and Ellen. Three other shirts, each a different color, were lying in a pile on the counter at Hang Ten—a store in downtown Sweet Valley that specialized in clothes for surfers.

"Which one do you like best?" he asked. "This blue one? Or the red one with the waves on it?"

Since their visit to the beach the day before, all Christoph could talk about was becoming a surfer— or at least looking like one. The exhibition that night didn't start until seven o'clock, so Jessica, Lila, and Ellen brought him to Hang Ten right after school.

"I think the blue one is you," Lila said.

"Definitely," Ellen agreed. "It matches your eyes. "

"I don't know . . ." Jessica said, biting her lower lip in thought. "I think red might be your color."

"Then it is settled," Christoph said, beaming. "I'll take both!"

As they walked out of the shop, Bruno ran up to them. It looked as if he'd been jogging by himself.

"Ah, Christoph," Bruno said. "I have been looking all over for you. The exhibition tonight has been changed from seven o'clock to eight o'clock. Coach Schmidt asked me to tell everyone."

Christoph merely nodded, and Bruno jogged away without another word.

"Great! That gives us an extra hour of shopping, Christoph," Lila said. "Let's go to the mall!"

"Even though the exhibition doesn't start until eight, I still want to be there an hour early," Christoph said. "I want to perform well tonight, and to do that I must warm up properly."

But when Jessica, Christoph, Lila, and Ellen walked into the gym at Sweet Valley Middle School at exactly seven o'clock that night, Christoph stopped dead in his tracks. His eyes opened wide, and his jaw dropped in horror.

"Oh, no!" he cried.

"What's wrong, Christoph?" Lila asked worriedly.

Jessica looked around and quickly saw what was wrong: all the other East German gymnasts were out on the floor getting ready to begin the exhibition. Christoph was late! His fellow teammates were gathered in the center of the gym, waiting for their names to be announced to the crowd.

"I thought Bruno said the exhibition started at eight tonight," Jessica remarked.

"He did," Christoph said, shaking his head. "I shouldn't have believed him!"

"Maybe if you hurry and get out there, Coach Schmidt won't be too angry," Jessica said.

"Hurry, Christoph," Lila urged him.

Christoph ran toward the locker room without looking back.

Jessica found Elizabeth, Amy, and Julie sitting by the team's bench. The gym was filled to capacity. The local newspaper had run a front-page article about the exhibition, and the people of Sweet Valley had turned out in droves. Luckily Elizabeth and her friends had saved seats for them. Before Jessica could even sit down, the three girls greeted her with a flurry of questions.

"Where's Christoph?" Elizabeth said. "Is he all right?"

"The exhibition's about to begin," Amy said. "We've been so worried."

"What happened?" Julie asked.

Jessica looked at her sister, then glanced angrily down the end of the bench at Bruno.

"That creep Bruno told Christoph that the exhibition was changed to eight o'clock," Jessica said. "We would have been on time if it hadn't been for Bruno!"

A few seconds later, Christoph came rushing out of the locker room and took his place with his teammates on the bench. Coach Schmidt immediately walked over and stood before him.

"I see you are not taking these exhibitions very

seriously, Christoph," the coach said with barely concealed anger. "I am very disappointed in you."

"But Coach Schmidt," Christoph began, "I can explain . . ."

Coach Schmidt cut him off with a wave of his hand.

"There is no need to explain," he said. "All of your teammates were here on time. Obviously the stories I have been hearing about you are true. I must take disciplinary action. You will not be allowed to perform tonight."

"What?" Christoph demanded. "But I need to work out tonight if I am to be ready for the competition tomorrow night," he cried. "This is not fair! You should allow me to explain." He glared angrily at Bruno, who was watching from the other end of the bench.

"I don't need explanations," Coach Schmidt said. "I am the coach of this team, and you will do as I say."

Coach Schmidt turned and walked away without giving Christoph a chance to say another word.

Christoph remained on the bench while the rest of his teammates put on the exhibition for the crowd. He hung his head and barely watched the others. Bruno, as if spurred on by Christoph's misfortune, performed magnificently. As he wound up his last routine the crowd gave him a rousing ovation.

After the exhibition was over, Bruno walked over and stood before Christoph. "It looks as if I am the best gymnast on the team now," he sneered. "All I must do is win the competition tomorrow night, and I will be number one. Your father will be very disappointed in you. Too bad you were late, Christoph."

With that, he grabbed his warm-up jacket and walked across the gym floor toward the locker room.

At home later that night, the twins and Steven tried to convince Christoph that he should tell the coach about the dirty trick Bruno had played on him. But Christoph wouldn't hear of it.

"You've got to say something to the coach," Elizabeth pleaded.

"What Bruno is doing to you isn't fair," Steven said. "He's making you look bad just so he can look good. You should tell the coach right away."

Christoph shook his head. "No," he said sadly. "Coach Schmidt believes that my heart isn't in this. All I can do is make sure that I win the competition tomorrow night. That is the one that means a great deal. I must take first place. It is the only way I can change his mind."

"But Bruno will only get worse," Jessica insisted. "If you don't put a stop to it, he'll just keep on doing things to get you in trouble."

Christoph merely shrugged. "I'd rather just forget about it," he said. "Thursday night's competition is the only thing that matters now. I still think that I am better than Bruno. By the way, Elizabeth," Christoph added, obviously anxious to change the subject, "I read the article you wrote about me, and I think it's great. You almost make me sound too good!"

Elizabeth beamed. "I'm glad you like it," she said. "I had more fun writing your story than any other."

"I liked the part about how much I like America," Christoph said. "It's really true. My country is nice, but America is the place to be."

"Hey, take a look at this," Steven said, pointing to the TV. "An East German ballet dancer defected to America yesterday. Do you know him, Christoph?"

Elizabeth turned up the sound on the television and watched as the reporter told of how the dancer had left his wife and young daughter behind in East Germany. "How can anyone even think of doing that?" she said sadly. "I mean, leaving your whole family and not knowing if you'll ever see them again . . ."

Steven laughed. "Are you kidding? If it meant getting away from you two, I'd do it in a second!"

Jessica laughed, but Elizabeth just frowned at Steven and shook her head.

"It was just a joke," Steven said. "Really."

Elizabeth noticed an uncomfortable look cross Christoph's face as he watched the report. Using the remote control, he quickly switched the channel to a game show.

"I'm getting worried about you, Christoph. You watch too many of these shows. They'll turn your brain to mush!"

Christoph laughed as he switched through the channels. "I've never seen so many different shows," he said. "It would probably take me years to understand all the programs here in America," he admitted. "I'd sure like to stay here and try, though."

The same uncomfortable look returned to Christoph's face. And Elizabeth couldn't help but wonder exactly what it meant.

Seven

◇

"Finished!" Elizabeth cried. She pulled the first copy of the latest *Sweet Valley Sixers* off the mimeograph machine and held it up for Amy, Brooke, and Julie to see. Elizabeth and her fellow reporters were in Mr. Bowman's office after school on Thursday.

"Yea!" Amy and Brooke shouted. They congratulated one another with pats on the back.

"I wasn't sure we'd finish on time," Elizabeth admitted. "This is the longest issue we've ever done, and in the shortest time, too."

"Well, we did it!" Brooke exclaimed.

"Let's double the number of copies we print," Julie said. "Everyone on the East German squad said they want to bring home extra copies for their families."

Elizabeth brought the paper over to Mr. Bowman's desk for him to see. Mr. Bowman, the faculty advisor of the *Sixers*, was one of Elizabeth's favorite teachers.

"Well, what do you think?" Mr. Bowman asked Elizabeth as he glanced through it quickly. "Should we start rehearsing our acceptance speeches for the Pulitzer prize?"

"I don't know about that," Elizabeth said. "But I think we've definitely outdone ourselves this time."

After the remaining copies of the paper had been run off, Elizabeth placed one in her bookbag.

"I have to go," she said. "I'll see you guys tonight at the competition."

That night the gym was filled with students from both the high school and the middle school. Elizabeth and Amy came in and sat with Jessica and Lila.

When the gymnasts finished their warm-ups, they gathered around Coach Schmidt for last-minute instructions. Christoph, however, stood outside the group, his head lowered.

"What's the matter with Christoph?" Elizabeth asked. "He doesn't look ready for a big competition."

"I think he's really worried," Steven answered, shaking his head. "If he doesn't do well, he could be in real trouble. And not being able to practice last night seemed to really upset him."

Ms. Langberg and Coach Cassels had come over from the middle school to judge the events along with Coach Schmidt and the two East German assistant coaches.

The competition began with the floor exercises, and Viktor was the first to compete. He raced from one end of the mat to the other with lightning speed, performing daring flips, somersaults, and handstands with ease. He concluded his routine with a double back flip. He held his hands in the air proudly as the crowd cheered.

Coach Cassels, the middle school basketball coach, and Ms. Langberg each awarded Viktor 9.6's for his routine. The East German judges each gave him a 9.5.

Bruno was next. Though he was much bigger than Viktor, he performed his moves with the same speed and agility. His routine consisted of the most difficult moves, and he performed them brilliantly. When he finished, two judges gave him a 9.8 and the other three a 9.9. Bruno strode arrogantly back to the bench.

After all the others had performed, it was Christoph's turn. The crowd cheered loudly when his name was announced.

"C'mon, Christoph!" Elizabeth yelled as loudly as she could.

But in spite of the warm reception he received, it was obvious once he began his routine that he wasn't at his best. His moves were sloppy and hesitant. After a series of difficult back handsprings, he landed near the edge of the mat and almost fell. When he finished, the crowd applauded politely. Christoph walked off the mat with his head down, obviously unhappy with his performance.

When the judges displayed their scores, the twins, Steven, and their friends groaned. Coach Cassels gave Christoph a 9.2, and the others awarded him 9.3's. They were the lowest scores received by anyone so far.

"Oh, no," Jessica moaned. "Bruno's way ahead already. Christoph's got to start doing well."

"Maybe he just had trouble with the floor exercises," Steven said hopefully. "The side horse is next. That's one of his strongest events."

But Christoph's routine on the side horse left little doubt that he wasn't in peak form. His routine normally was smooth and rapid. But tonight he was slower, and his usually spectacular dismount seemed sluggish. The judges awarded scores ranging from 9.1 to 9.4.

Bruno, who had received 9.8's from all the judges, was even further ahead now. Sitting on the bench, Christoph seemed more discouraged than before.

By the time the horizontal bar and long horse events were over, Bruno had a commanding lead. He seemed to get stronger with each event, while Christoph only appeared to get more discouraged.

"I've got to say something to him," Elizabeth said when there was a break in the action.

She walked down to the bench. Christoph had his face buried in a towel. He looked up and smiled weakly when he saw Elizabeth.

"Christoph, what's wrong?" she asked. "This is the most important competition of all. It looks like you're not even trying."

Christoph shrugged. "I am trying," he insisted. "But it is no use. I am way behind. Coach Schmidt will tell my father how badly I performed."

"But you're the best gymnast on this team," Elizabeth said. "Letting Bruno upset you like this isn't right. You've got to prove to everyone that you are still the best."

Jessica and Steven came down and joined Elizabeth.

"Please, Christoph," Jessica said. "Everyone in the gym knows that you're really the best. Didn't you hear the way everyone cheered for you?"

Christoph nodded slowly.

"Don't give up," Steven urged. "You can't let Bruno do this to you."

"We're behind you, Christoph," Elizabeth said.

The twins and Steven climbed back up to their seats in the bleachers as Viktor began the second to last event. "Do you think he believed us?" Jessica asked.

"I don't know," Elizabeth said with a sigh. "We'll just have to wait to find out."

Viktor performed magnificently on the rings, getting scores of 9.7 and 9.8 from the judges. Bruno followed. His great strength made the rings one of his best events. His perfectly executed straight body cross sent the crowd into thunderous applause, but a slipup on his dismount gave him five scores of 9.7.

Then it was Christoph's turn. As he began his routine, it was clear to Elizabeth that their pep talk had cheered him up. His routine was brilliant. He performed the difficult moves to perfection, including a somersault into a handstand and a straight body cross that was even better than Bruno's. When he finished with a double back somersault dismount, he was the crowd favorite once again. And when the judges gave him a series of 9.9's, everyone in the gym started chanting his name.

Christoph walked back to the bench with a huge grin on his face. He gave a quick wave to the twins and Steven.

"The parallel bars are next," Steven said excitedly.

"That's Christoph's best event," Elizabeth said, biting her lip.

Bruno was still in first place, followed by Viktor in second and Konrad in third. Christoph, because of his slow start, was a distant fifth. With only one event to go, it was impossible for Christoph to catch up to Bruno.

One after another, the gymnasts performed their routines. The parallel bars were not Bruno's best event, but he performed with great skill. When it was over, he received four 9.6's and a 9.7 from the judges—enough to keep him in first place.

Then came Christoph's turn. He walked over to the bars and began his routine without hesitation. With the crowd cheering him on, he went through a series of magnificent spins and turns. He performed handstands and back flips flawlessly. His dismount, a handstand into a backward somersault, was perfect. He walked back to the bench and was greeted with handshakes and high-fives from Viktor, Dieter, Oskar, and Max.

"That was fantastic!" Elizabeth cried.

The competition was over. Coach Schmidt and the other judges gathered around a table. When they were through tallying the scores for each gymnast, Ms. Langberg stepped up to the microphone to announce the winners.

"Quiet down, everyone," Ms. Langberg said.

Elizabeth looked at Jessica and crossed her fingers.

"First place goes to Bruno Heiling," Ms. Langberg announced. "In second place, Viktor Schneider. And in third place, Christoph Beckmann.

"At this point I'd like to thank the East German gymnasts and their coaches for coming to Sweet Valley," Ms. Langberg continued. "It's been a great week! See you all at the dance tomorrow night at the middle school."

The twins and Steven rushed down to the bench as the crowd gave all the gymnasts a round of applause.

"You were great, Christoph!" Elizabeth exclaimed. "Your parallel bars routine was incredible."

But when Christoph gazed at the twins and Steven, he didn't look pleased.

"This is the most horrible night of my life," he said.

"You shouldn't say that, Christoph," Elizabeth said. "After all that's happened, you did very well."

"Elizabeth's right," Jessica said. "You're still the best. The whole crowd loved you. You should be proud of yourself."

"I am glad that the crowd liked me," Christoph said sadly. "But my father certainly will not be proud. With him, it is all or nothing." He picked up his towel and started for the locker room.

The twins and Steven watched him walk across the gym. "I wish there was something we could do to cheer him up," Elizabeth said.

"Maybe the dance tomorrow night will make him feel better," Jessica said, shrugging.

"I don't know," Steven said. "It looks like the only thing that will cheer him up is a first-place finish for his father, but it's too late for that."

Eight

◇

The following night, Lila and Ellen covered Jessica's eyes and led her into the gym at Sweet Valley Middle School. When they removed their hands, Jessica gazed around her in wonder.

"Wow!" she exclaimed. "It's fantastic!"

The gym was covered from floor to ceiling with red, white, and blue streamers to represent the American flag, and red, yellow, and black balloons, the colors of the East German flag. A mirrored ball was spinning slowly, reflecting tiny points of light all around the gym ceiling. Up on a platform, Johnny Gordon and the Waves, a popular local band, were playing one of Jessica's favorite Melody Power songs.

"Wow," she said, "The decorating committee really did a great job!"

"We've got a table saved just for the Unicorns right over near the band," Lila said as she and Ellen led Jessica through the gym.

Janet and Tamara were already sitting at the Unicorns' table.

"When is Christoph coming?" Janet asked anxiously. "I can't wait until he sees his gift."

"He should be here any minute," Jessica replied. "All of the gymnasts are coming in together."

In the meantime, Elizabeth arrived with Amy, Julie, and Ken Matthews. They found seats at a table next to the Unicorns and waited for Christoph and the rest of the East German students to arrive.

When Mr. Clark, the school's principal, stepped up to the microphone, everyone quieted down.

"I'd like to thank you all for making this a very successful visit," he said. "Now, let's give the East German team a big round of applause to show how much we appreciate their coming here!"

Everyone stood and cheered as Coach Schmidt led the gymnastics team into the middle of the floor and out onto the platform. Bruno was right behind Coach Schmidt, and Christoph was the last in line, walking behind Oskar and Max.

"It reminds me of the first time we saw them at the airport," Amy said to Elizabeth.

"It's hard to believe that the week has already gone by," Elizabeth said sadly.

She watched Christoph standing with the other members of his squad. She knew he was sad about leaving. But worse than that, it seemed as if he still hadn't gotten over his loss to Bruno.

"There's plenty of food and refreshments," Mr. Clark added, interrupting Elizabeth's thoughts. "Everyone have a great time!"

The East German students walked off the stage and into the crowd. Christoph, Viktor, Max, and Oskar wandered over to the Unicorns' table. They were immediately greeted with a barrage of hugs and tearful goodbyes.

"I can't believe you're leaving tomorrow," Lila said to Christoph. "Do you promise to write?"

"It seems like you just got here yesterday," Ellen said. She looked down at Christoph's gift, which she was clutching in her hands. "I was supposed to wait until the end of the night to give you this, but I can't. This is from all the Unicorns."

"Open it!" Viktor said happily.

Christoph took the package and opened it. Inside was a pair of beautiful rosewood drumsticks.

"Read what it says on them," Lila said excitedly.

Christoph looked closely at the sticks and read aloud: "To Christoph with love from the Unicorns."

It was clear that the present had taken Christoph by surprise. "The drumsticks are fantastic. Thank you," he said. "You have all been so nice to me. I am going to miss you very much."

Elizabeth looked around the table. Tears were in everyone's eyes. In only a week, Christoph had become a real friend.

"Please excuse me for a moment," Christoph said, turning suddenly and walking away.

"I'll be right back," Elizabeth said to Jessica. She followed Christoph through the crowded gym. When she caught up with him outside, he was twirling his new drumsticks.

"That's pretty good," Elizabeth said. "I'll bet that took a lot of practice."

"Yes, it did," Christoph said. "Unfortunately, that won't do me much good."

"What are you talking about?"

"When I get home, my father will probably make me give up the drums. I was hoping I could convince him to let me join a band, but I'm sure he won't allow it now."

"I don't understand," Elizabeth said. "Can't your father see that gymnastics is only a game?"

Christoph laughed bitterly. "Maybe to other people it's only a game," he said. "To my father, it is more!"

"Why don't we go back to the dance," Elizabeth said quickly, trying to take Christoph's mind away from his father. "You should enjoy your last night here."

Christoph nodded weakly and followed Elizabeth back into the gym.

"What's the matter?" Jessica asked Elizabeth when Christoph went off to get a soda.

"There's no time to explain," Elizabeth replied grimly. "Tonight must be the best night of Christoph's trip," she said. "We can't let him go home feeling so sad."

"What can we do?" Jessica asked. "It looks like it would take a miracle to get him to smile."

Elizabeth thought for a moment. Suddenly her eyes lit up. "I've got an idea!" she said. "You dance with him. I'll be right back."

"What have you got up your sleeve?" Jessica asked, looking suspiciously at her twin.

"Don't worry," Elizabeth said casually as she got up from the table. "You just get Christoph to dance. I'll take care of the rest." With that, she raced off into the crowd.

A minute later, Christoph returned, holding a can of soda.

"Time to dance," Jessica said abruptly. She took the soda out of his hand, and pulled him out on the floor, ignoring his surprised look. "Come on, listen to that beat! I'm sure you're a terrific dancer!"

The band was pounding out an infectious rhythm, and Christoph began to dance. Jessica shouted as Christoph started to feel the beat. When the band finally stopped for a break after two more songs, Jessica and Christoph were grateful for the chance to catch their breath.

Just then Johnny Gordon, the band's lead singer, stepped up to the microphone. "I have an announcement to make," he said, and immediately everyone quieted down. "We've got a special guest in the audience tonight. His name is Christoph Beckmann, and I hear he's a really great drummer. Let's get him up here to do a song with us!"

The crowd roared and started to clap.

Christoph stood on the dance floor in shock. He turned a deep shade of red.

"Get up there, Christoph!" Max cried.

"Show everyone how good you are!" Oskar yelled.

Finally Christoph, grinning from ear to ear, climbed onto the platform and spoke briefly with Johnny Gordon. Then he sat down behind the drums. He was clearly thrilled by the chance to play with a band.

"Christoph's a big Johnny Buck fan," Johnny shouted to the crowd. "So here we go."

Johnny counted to four, and the band, Christoph included, roared into one of Johnny Buck's biggest hits, "Dreamer."

"So this is what you had planned! You're a genius!" Jessica shouted enthusiastically. "Christoph will remember this night forever!"

As the song continued, the twins danced, looking at Christoph the whole time. He pounded away on the drums as though he had been playing with the band for years.

When the song came to a rousing finish, Christoph stood behind the drums and raised his arms triumphantly.

"You were wonderful!" Elizabeth exclaimed when he came down from the platform.

"I have always wanted to play with a band. It was fantastic!" Christoph said, still smiling brightly.

As the twins and Christoph made their way back to the Unicorn table, the rest of the East German team met them. They hooted and hollered and clapped Christoph on the back. Only one member of the team was missing.

"Look," Elizabeth said to Jessica. She nudged Jessica and nodded toward the back of the room. "Bruno doesn't look too happy, does he?"

From across the room the twins could see Bruno putting on his coat and getting ready to leave.

"Should we tell Christoph?" Jessica wondered out loud.

"No," Elizabeth said, shaking her head. "Even mentioning Bruno's name on a night like tonight would be a big-mistake."

Nine

◇

On Saturday morning, Steven was shooting baskets out on the driveway. "Where's Christoph?" Jessica asked. "I thought you two would be playing basketball until he had to leave."

The flight that was to take the East German team back home was scheduled to leave at noon that day. A van was supposed to pick up Christoph at ten-thirty.

"I thought he'd be up, too," Steven replied with a shrug. "But when I got up he was still sleeping. I guess he's pretty tired."

"That's strange," Jessica said.

Jessica went back upstairs, hoping to see Christoph up and about. Instead, when she looked into Steven's room, she saw Christoph sitting up in bed. Mrs. Wakefield was holding her hand on his forehead, and Elizabeth was on the other side of the bed, wringing out a damp cloth.

"What's wrong?" Jessica asked, alarmed.

Christoph tried to answer, but couldn't seem to manage more than a mumble.

"Christoph's not feeling well," Mrs. Wakefield said. "Your father already called for Coach Schmidt and the doctor. They should be here any minute."

When the doctor and Coach Schmidt arrived, the twins and their parents were ushered out of Steven's room so the doctor could examine Christoph.

"I'm sure this won't take very long," the doctor said. "If you'll excuse us, please."

"Do you think it's serious, Mom?" Jessica asked, as the Wakefields went downstairs into the living room.

"Well, he was complaining of stomach pains," she said. "It could be a stomach virus, but I guess we'll have to wait and see."

It seemed like forever before Coach Schmidt and the doctor appeared.

"Is Christoph OK?" Jessica asked anxiously.

"He's got a virus, but he is going to be fine," the doctor said.

"Mr. and Mrs. Wakefield, I would like to ask you a question," Coach Schmidt said, obviously troubled by something. "Christoph must not be moved for a couple of days—certainly he cannot fly right away. Would it be possible for him to stay here for a few more days?"

"That's no problem at all," Mr. Wakefield said. "We'd be happy to have Christoph stay. You can be sure that he'll be well taken care of."

"Very well," the coach said. "The rest of the team is going home today, but I have a seminar in San Francisco that I must attend. I will return on Thursday afternoon. Christoph will certainly be better by then, and we will fly home together."

After Coach Schmidt and the doctor had left, the twins started upstairs.

"Hold on there a minute," Mrs. Wakefield said, shaking her head. "What Christoph needs right now is rest. Let's let him sleep a little while, OK?"

The twins marched glumly down the stairs and into the living room. "I hope he gets up soon," Jessica said. "It won't be much fun having him here if he's sick!"

"Is that for Christoph, Mom?" Elizabeth asked.

She had spent most of the day looking for an excuse to check on him. Jessica had grown tired of waiting and had gone to Lila's house to work on a new cheer with the Boosters.

"Yes, it is," Mrs. Wakefield answered, pouring out a bowl of chicken soup.

"Can I check on him now?" Elizabeth said, getting up from the table. "Please. I've been waiting all day!"

"OK, but—"

Before she could say any more, Elizabeth had darted out of the kitchen and up the stairs. She knocked lightly on the door to Steven's room, then opened it slowly.

Christoph was awake, but looked sleepy. "How are you feeling?" she asked softly. He smiled weakly.

"OK, I guess. My stomach's a little queasy, though."

"Here, have some water," she said, handing him a glass of water that was on the night table. "I just finished reading all about Florence Nightingale," she added with a smile, "so you're being taken care of by an expert."

"Christoph will be up and about in no time," Elizabeth said cheerfully as her mother walked in a few minutes later with the hot soup. "Maybe he'll be able to go outside tomorrow and get some fresh air."

But despite all the signs that Christoph was getting over his illness, he remained in bed, refusing to eat, for the entire weekend.

"I thought for sure he'd be feeling much better by now," Elizabeth said to Jessica on Monday night. "He's been sick for three whole days."

Jessica nodded grimly. "I know. I'm worried, too. I wonder if he's ever going to get better."

"I thought you said there was some chocolate cake left over," Jessica said, poking her head into the refrigerator. She had been looking forward to a piece of her mother's famous dark chocolate cake all day Tuesday.

Mrs. Wakefield walked into the kitchen. "I'm sure there was a piece in there this morning, honey," she said. "Maybe Steven ate it when he got home from school."

"But I wanted that piece," Jessica complained.

"Hi, everybody! I'm home!" Elizabeth yelled as she walked in the front door. "What's going on?" she said, coming into the kitchen and seeing Jessica's glum expression. "You look like you just lost your best friend."

"Steven the Pig has struck again!" Jessica cried. "He ate the last piece of chocolate cake."

"You should do something about him, Mom," Elizabeth said, shaking her head. "Yesterday I went to get some oatmeal cookies while I was doing my homework, and the whole package was gone! I didn't even get one cookie!"

"I guess you're right," said Mrs. Wakefield. "I'll talk to him when he gets back from dinner at the Howells'. After all, I can't have either of you starving to death." She tousled Elizabeth's hair playfully and went back into the living room.

After dinner, Elizabeth went to straighten up Steven's room while Christoph took a shower. She was beginning to worry about him. Aside from the fact that he was still sick and refusing to eat, he spent most of his time in bed watching television. That night he'd come down to dinner, but not eaten a single bite of food.

Elizabeth picked up a pile of clothes from the floor and threw them into the hamper. As she was fluffing Christoph's pillow, she caught sight of something stuffed down between the headboard and the mattress. She reached down and pulled out an empty package of oatmeal cookies. It was the very same kind of cookies she had been searching for the day before.

Elizabeth decided that she had better look under the bed as well. To her surprise, she discovered a plate with a few crumbs of chocolate cake on it. So it was Christoph who'd taken the cake out of the refrigerator!

"We have to talk, Jess," Elizabeth said, rushing into her twin's room. She set the cookie bag and the cake plate down on Jessica's bed.

"Lizzie, why are you dumping all that garbage on my bed?" she asked. "I just finished making it."

"It's not garbage," Elizabeth said seriously. "I just discovered where all the chocolate cake went."

"Steven confessed?" Jessica asked delightedly. "Great!"

"Wrong, Jess," Elizabeth said. "It was Christoph. I found this plate under his bed and the cookie package behind the mattress."

"What?" Jessica cried in astonishment. "But how—"

Elizabeth shook her head. "Something tells me Christoph isn't as sick as he says he is."

Jessica's jaw dropped. "What should we do?"

"We should talk to him and find out what's going on."

The twins waited in their room while Christoph finished taking his shower. When they heard him turn the television on in his room, they marched across the hall and knocked on the door.

"Come in," Christoph called.

When the twins walked in, Christoph gave a little smile. "Oh, hello," he said weakly. "I thought maybe we could go to the Dairi Burger tonight, but I'm not feeling very well."

Elizabeth set the plate and the cookie package in front of Christoph. He stared at the floor guiltily.

"Christoph, what's going on?" Elizabeth asked quietly. "You're not really sick anymore, are you?"

Christoph lowered his eyes.

"You are right. I don't feel sick anymore," Christoph admitted. "I really *was* sick, but only the first day. I've been sneaking cake and cookies when no one's around." He looked at the twins. "The only thing I am sick about now is that I must go home. I don't ever want to go back to East Germany!"

"You can't be serious, Christoph!" Elizabeth exclaimed. "What about your family? They'd miss you terribly."

Christoph began to pace around the room. It was clear from his angry expression that he wasn't joking. "They are the reason I don't want to go!"

he cried. "All they do is push me to train harder. They have taken all the fun out of it. I am tired of people telling me what to do. I like Sweet Valley. I'm going to stay here!"

The twins looked at each other, shocked.

"Christoph," Elizabeth said, her heart pounding. "You don't mean you want to—"

"That's exactly what I mean!" Christoph interrupted. "I am going to defect, and no one can stop me!"

Ten

◇

"Wow!" Steven exclaimed when Jessica told him the news. "Defecting! What a great idea."

"Steven, we've got to do something about this," Elizabeth explained. "We talked to him for over an hour but he just won't listen. It wouldn't be right for Christoph to stay here. He's got a family in East Germany that loves him."

"I think it would be great," Steven said. "A few lessons from me, and Christoph and I could be on the basketball team together."

"Come on, Steven!" Jessica warned. "Be serious! Coach Schmidt is coming back Thursday af-

ternoon. That means we've got less than two days
to make Christoph change his mind."

Steven nodded slowly. "You're right," he said,
suddenly grasping the seriousness of the situa-
tion. "Maybe I should talk to him."

"That's a great idea," Elizabeth said. "He might
listen to you."

Steven was about to knock on the door to his
room, when Mr. Wakefield ran up the stairs.

"There's a phone call for Christoph," Mr. Wakefield announced. "It's his mother calling from East
Germany."

Christoph came out of his room and looked at
the twins and Steven, a nervous expression on his
face. Jessica watched as Christoph walked downstairs to take the call in Mr. Wakefield's study.
Then she ran to the phone extension in the hall-
way and reached for the receiver.

"Jess, what are you doing?" Elizabeth cried.

"Shh!" Jessica held a finger to her lips. She
picked up the receiver and quietly covered the
mouthpiece with her palm.

"Hello?" said Christoph.

Jessica heard Christoph's mother speaking German, but Christoph quickly interrupted her.

"I'm sorry, but I am going to be an American

now," he said sternly. "You must speak to me in English!"

"Christoph, I was so worried when I found out you didn't return home," his mother said, speaking in English now. "I hope you are feeling better. Are you being well taken care of?"

"There is no need to worry about me," Christoph said. "I can take care of myself. I don't ever want to return to East Germany. This is my home now. I will be able to do all the things I have dreamed of."

"Why are you talking like this?" his mother said. She sounded as though she might begin to cry.

"I don't want to talk anymore," Christoph said flatly. "I must go now."

"Please, Christoph," his mother said sadly. "I just want to see you. Gretchen and Ingrid miss you so much. We are sorry you won't make it home in time for your birthday tomorrow. We will have a big celebration when you get home."

"I must go now," Christoph repeated. "Goodbye."

"Christoph, wait," his mother pleaded. "Your father is not home now, but I will discuss this with him tonight. I know he will want to speak to you about this matter. He will call you tomorrow night. I hope you will think things over and feel better tomorrow.''

Christoph hung up the phone and marched out of the kitchen. He raced upstairs, and into Steven's room, slamming the door, without so much as a glance at the twins or Steven.

"Dad? Can we talk to you?" Elizabeth asked as the twins and Steven came into the living room. "We've got a problem."

"Sure," Mr. Wakefield said. "Is it serious?"

"We think so," Jessica said.

"Why don't we get your mother in here then," Mr. Wakefield said, getting up from the couch. "I think she should hear this, too."

A few minutes later, their parents were sitting together, listening patiently as Elizabeth and Jessica described everything that had happened, including Christoph's decision to defect.

"I can hardly believe that Christoph would even consider such a move," Mrs. Wakefield said. "Do you think he's serious?"

The twins nodded in unison.

"Maybe you should have a talk with him, Ned," Mrs. Wakefield said.

Mr. Wakefield nodded. "I think you're right,"

he said. "I wouldn't want him to make any rash decisions."

"Wait!" Jessica cried. "I've got an idea. It's Christoph's birthday tomorrow."

"But what good is that going to do us?" Mrs. Wakefield asked.

"What if we throw a surprise party for him?" Jessica said. "If we do it right, we can make him feel so homesick he'll forget about defecting."

"We can remind him of his parents, his sisters, and his friends who are back home," Elizabeth added.

Mr. and Mrs. Wakefield looked at each other for a moment. Finally, Mr. Wakefield nodded.

"You may be right," he said. "But I think we'll need to call Christoph's parents tonight as well. I don't think we're going to be able to do this all on our own. We're going to need their help, too."

"Look what I found!" Steven yelled as he burst through the kitchen door. He unrolled a colorful poster of an old cobblestoned street in Berlin. "Mrs. Reiter, the German teacher at school, said I could borrow it. What do you think?"

"That's great, Steven," Elizabeth said. "I think it would look great hanging by the front door."

It was after school on Wednesday and preparations for Christoph's surprise party were in full swing. Amy and Ken were in the living room putting together a collage of photographs that showed Christoph with his teammates. There were even a few photographs of Christoph's house in East Germany that he had left lying around in his room.

Julie, Brooke, Ellen, and Tamara were blowing up balloons and hanging streamers throughout the house.

Lila was at the stereo trying to find just the right song to play the moment Christoph walked in. Jessica had stopped by the library on the way home and had taken out a recording of traditional German music.

Elizabeth and her mother were busy carrying delicious-smelling German foods like strudel and Wiener schnitzel from the kitchen to the dining room table. Mrs. Wakefield had been cooking practically all day long.

"What time is it?" Lila asked excitedly. "We must be running out of time." Steven and Mr. Wakefield had taken Christoph to a varsity basketball game at Sweet Valley High in order to keep him away from the house.

Elizabeth looked at her watch. "It's almost seven! They'll be here in five minutes. Let's hurry!"

"It's kind of funny, isn't it?" Brooke said to Elizabeth. "All this so Christoph will *leave* us! I wish it was the other way around. Even though I know what we're doing is right, it would be great if he could stay here."

"I know," Elizabeth said. "Before Christoph started to talk about defecting, all I could think of was how great it would be if he lived in Sweet Valley."

"Here they come!" Julie exclaimed a few minutes later.

Everyone took their places in the living room and waited for Christoph. Elizabeth couldn't wait to see the look on his face when he walked through the door.

"Surprise!" everyone shouted when Christoph arrived.

"Happy birthday, Christoph!" Elizabeth said.

Christoph's eyes widened and a gigantic smile spread across his face.

"How did you know it was my birthday?" he asked in astonishment. "This is fantastic!"

"How about some music?" Lila said. She turned on the stereo and a traditional German song began to play.

Christoph stood absolutely still for a moment, unable to speak. "I—I—don't know what to say," he stammered. "I'd still like to know how you knew . . ."

His voice trailed off as Elizabeth took him by the arm and led him into the dining room. She winked at Jessica, whose face was glowing. Elizabeth was sure their plan was going to work.

Christoph took one look at the dining room table and his eyes almost popped out of his head.

"Strudel!" he cried in delight. He picked up a slice of the pastry and took a bite. "This is my absolute favorite. How did you know?"

Mrs. Wakefield smiled cheerfully and shrugged. "Lucky guess, I suppose," she said.

When Lila replaced the German songs with a Johnny Buck album, the party really took off. Julie and Ellen passed around a tray full of sodas and snacks, and Ken and Steven brought a bundle of gift-wrapped packages into the living room for Christoph to open.

All the while, Christoph wandered around the room, amazed at all the trouble the Wakefields and their friends had gone through to make his birthday a happy one. He stopped and stared at the collage of photographs that Ken and Amy had put together. Elizabeth saw the smile on his face disappear for a moment, replaced instead by a wistful gaze.

"I wonder what Oskar and Viktor are doing today?" Elizabeth said.

"I was wondering that, too," Christoph said, his eyes suddenly moist. "And Gretchen and Ingrid . . ."

When the phone rang a few minutes later, Jessica picked up the receiver. She motioned for everyone to be quiet.

"Christoph, it's for you," she announced. "It's your father."

Christoph looked startled for a moment. Jessica held the phone out for him and saw the flicker of indecision in his eyes. Would Christoph refuse to talk to his father? If he did, the plan might be ruined.

"May I take it in the study?" he asked.

"Of course," Mr. Wakefield said. "Go right ahead."

"What do you think is going to happen?" Julie whispered to Elizabeth when Christoph left the room.

Elizabeth shrugged. Her only hope was that Christoph's father would be more understanding about his future.

A few minutes later, Christoph came back into the living room. He stared down at the floor without saying a word.

"Is everything OK, Christoph?" Mrs. Wakefield asked.

Christoph nodded. "I have an announcement to make," he began. "I am very grateful for my birthday party. You have made me feel at home here. But without *my* family, I will never really be home. You are the nicest people I have ever met. I had decided to stay here in America, but even though I love it here, it would not be the same without my mother and father and Gretchen and Ingrid. So I am going to return to East Germany tomorrow with Coach Schmidt."

The Wakefields looked at one another, smiling warmly. Their plan had worked even better than they hoped it would.

"I'm sure you made the right decision, Christoph," Mr. Wakefield said, patting him on the shoulder.

"Yes, I, too, am sure," Christoph agreed. There were tears in his eyes as he smiled at everyone.

"I hope everything works out OK, Christoph," Elizabeth said. "I hope your father understands how you feel now."

"I think he does," Christoph replied. "I will decide whether to continue my gymnastics training when I get home, and my father has promised to abide by my decision."

"That's wonderful, Christoph," Jessica said.

"Did Gretchen and Ingrid wish you happy birthday?" Julie asked.

Christoph beamed. "Yes," he answered. "And Ingrid slipped and told me what my birthday present from my father was."

"What is it?" Jessica squealed.

"A new drum set," Christoph said, beaming. "I can't wait to get home and play it."

"Well," Mrs. Wakefield said, "with all this excitement, I'll bet you must have quite an appetite."

"You bet!" Christoph said happily. "Besides, tomorrow I have a long flight home. And I remember how bad the food was on the way here. I'd better fill up tonight!"

Eleven

◇

"Christoph didn't leave yet, did he?" Jessica asked as she burst into the kitchen after school on Thursday. "Please tell me I'm not too late!"

Mrs. Wakefield looked up from the plate of strudel she was wrapping up and smiled. "You made it with time to spare," she said. "Everyone's upstairs in Steven's room."

Jessica climbed the stairs two at a time, clutching a paper bag in her hands.

"I was worried I might not see you before I left," Christoph said when Jessica burst in. "What happened to you?"

"There was something I had to do on the way home from school."

Jessica handed the brown paper bag to Christoph. He looked it over.

"Great wrapping paper," Steven teased.

"I didn't have time!" Jessica protested.

Christoph opened the bag and pulled out a copy of the newest Johnny Buck album, *Saturday Night Dancin'*.

"This is fantastic!" Christoph said. "I'll be the first one in East Germany to have this record! Thank you."

Just then, a car horn beeped out front.

"That must be Coach Schmidt," Christoph said quietly. "It's time to go."

Steven took one of Christoph's suitcases downstairs.

"Are you feeling better today, Christoph?" Coach Schmidt asked when the Wakefield family and their guest had gone outside and gathered around the car.

"Yes," Christoph answered. "I'm feeling fine now."

Coach Schmidt shook hands with Mr. and Mrs. Wakefield.

"Thank you for taking care of Christoph these

extra days," Coach Schmidt said. "We are very grateful to you."

"It was our pleasure," Mrs. Wakefield replied. "Christoph is a wonderful boy. We'd love to have him back."

Coach Schmidt nodded to everyone and started back to the car. "We have only a few minutes, Christoph," he said. "It is time to say goodbye."

"Mr. and Mrs. Wakefield, thank you for making me feel so at home these two weeks," Christoph said.

Christoph shook hands with Mr. Wakefield. Mrs. Wakefield smiled and handed him the wrapped-up strudel. "For your flight home," she said. "I hope Coach Schmidt likes strudel as well."

"He loves it," Christoph said.

Steven shook hands with Christoph.

"Thank you for showing me how to play basketball," Christoph said. "When I get home, I will try to practice. Who knows, maybe someday I will be as good a player as you."

Christoph turned to the twins.

"Have you decided whether you're going to continue with your gymnastics?" Elizabeth asked.

"I'm going to think about it for a while," he said. "If I stay on the team, there may be a chance we'll come back to Sweet Valley sometime. And as for reasons to stay on the team, that's the best of all!''

Later that night, Elizabeth was sitting at her desk, trying to concentrate on her math homework. Jessica was in her room. She was supposed to be doing homework as well, but all Elizabeth could hear was her sister singing along with the new Melody Power album, *Powerful*.

"Jess, can you keep it down, please?" Elizabeth called.

"What?" she heard Jessica call. "You'll have to come in here. I can't hear a word you're saying."

Elizabeth groaned. She dropped her pencil down on her notebook and got up from her desk.

"Jess, I'm trying to finish my homework."

"Don't I sound just like Melody?" Jessica shouted above the music.

"Sure, Jess," Elizabeth said, turning the volume down. "But I'm having a hard time concentrating on my homework."

"She's so fabulous," Jessica said, staring at the album cover. "She's giving a concert in Sweet Valley next week, but the tickets are already sold out."

Elizabeth walked back to her room to finish her

homework. Just as she sat down at her desk, the phone rang.

"Can you get that, Jess?" she called. "Mom and Dad are out back by the pool."

"I'm memorizing the words to Melody's songs," Jessica called back. "You get it."

"Jess, I'm doing homework. *Please.*"

But when the phone kept ringing, Elizabeth finally went out to the hall and answered it.

"Hi, this is Rockin' Jimmy Rocker, from KROK Radio," a loud voice came through the receiver. "Are there any Melody Power fans at home?"

Elizabeth could hardly speak. She had heard that one of the local radio stations was giving away tickets to the Melody Power concert. Could it be . . . ?

"Um, I love Melody Power," she said.

"Great!" Rockin' Jimmy Rocker shouted. "If you can answer the following question about Melody, you can win two free tickets to her concert next week. You'll have thirty seconds to answer. Are you ready?"

"I'm ready!" Elizabeth said. She quickly motioned for Jessica to come to the phone. "It's a radio station giving away free tickets to Melody's concert next week!" she said, her hand covering the mouthpiece.

Jessica dashed into the hall, her heart pounding. Elizabeth positioned the phone so that Jessica could also hear.

"What is the last line of Melody's latest hit single, 'Moon Walkin' Into My Heart'?" You've got thirty seconds."

In a matter of seconds Jessica ran into her room and picked up the album cover. She found the lyric sheet and rushed back to Elizabeth.

"Uh, 'Feels so good, feels so right, moon walkin' with you tonight!' " Elizabeth shouted into the phone.

"That's right!" Rockin' Jimmy Rocker shouted. "You've just won two tickets to next week's Melody Power concert in Sweet Valley!"

After giving the DJ her name and address, Elizabeth shrieked happily and danced around the room with Jessica.

"Gee, I wonder who I should take with me to the concert?" Elizabeth said when they finally settled down a few minutes later. "I can bring anyone I want . . ."

Jessica's jaw dropped and her eyes narrowed. "You wouldn't!" she shrieked. "I'm the one who gave you the answer! I'm just as responsible as you are for winning! And I want to be in a band just like Melody's. I'm going to be a famous rock star someday. You have to let me come with you, Elizabeth!"

Elizabeth smiled. "I was just kidding, Jess," she said. "I can't wait to tell everyone! You and I are going to the biggest concert of the year!"

Will Jessica's new ambition to sing in a band come true? Find out in Sweet Valley Twins #34, **JESSICA, THE ROCK STAR.**